ROSIE THE FARM TRUCK

by VICTORIA SCUDDER
Illustrated by KAM BAYO

Happy Reading!
Victoria

Scout & Company Publishing

For Jack

... my everything. I love you, buddy!

Mom

Rosie wakes with an extra bounce in her springs and revs her engine in excitement. Eight inches of fluffy white snow fell on Callahan Farm overnight and the ground is white and soft.

"What fun we will have with Farmer Jack today!" she announces. Rosie loves the snow!

Rosie zooms over to her friends as they finished gobbling up breakfast with Farmer Jack.

"Morning, Rosie!"

"Hi, everyone!"

She laughs while the chickens chase each other 'round and 'round in circles.

"I'll need extra help today," calls Farmer Jack. "A big storm is heading our way tomorrow night. The animals will need extra food, water, and blankets."

Rosie frowned. She really wanted to play in the snow with her friends.

"Don't be upset," whispers Scout the dog. "We'll all help, and then we'll have lots of time to play!"

Patches the horse chimes in.
"I'll even race you later, Rosie!"
She feels better already.

They quickly get to work. Rosie hauls extra hay to the barn. Then, she brings firewood to the main house and helps corral the cows in from the pasture.

George, the older draft horse, counts off each one to make sure none are missing. "Great teamwork!" praises Farmer Jack.

With the morning's work finished, everyone scatters to play.

"Go, Rosie, go!" cries Mr. Fiddlesticks, the bunny.

"Don't count me out, yet, Fiddlesticks," huffs Patches as he picks up the pace. Whooosh!

They almost skid across the finish line when Rosie
notices the two police cars up at the farmhouse.
"Uh-oh, this can't be good," she tells Frank. "It's
the twins. We'd better check on Farmer Jack!"

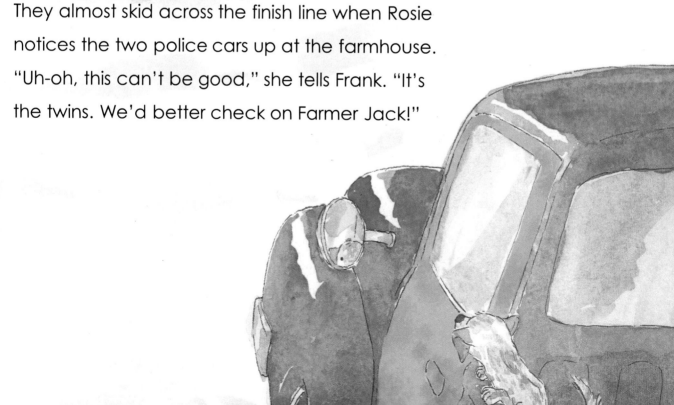

Steve and Tony are the town's finest police cars. They have been best friends with Rosie for as long as she can remember. They look so serious, and Rosie suddenly feels nervous.

"Official business, Red," they say. The mayor sent for you. She needs you in town right away.

Mayor Hope greets Rosie in Amaryllis Town Square.

"Thank you for meeting me so quickly," she says. She looks relieved to see Rosie.

"Is everything alright?" asks Rosie.

"A train broke down right outside of town, and it can't be fixed before tomorrow's storm. All of the passengers have been moved to warm shelters except those in two very special coaches. I need your help, Rosie," Mayor Hope tells her.

Rosie sees some of her friends and joins them while waiting for the mayor to take them to the train.

They arrive at the scene and are surprised to see four sweet reindeer poking their heads outside of the coaches. Rosie is confused. "How can we help these reindeer, Mayor Hope?"

"They were on their way to see a special teacher on the other side of the mountain. They want to learn how to read so that they can help Santa find the addresses that he needs to deliver toys to all the children," the Mayor explains.

Rosie moves toward the
reindeer to say hello. They look
sad. "What's wrong?" asks Rosie. "We'll
miss our classes and won't be able to help Santa in time,"
explains Trey, the oldest. "We can help you! But you'll need to come
with us," says Rosie.

Farmer Jack is waiting for Rosie back at Callahan Farm. She explains the problem and asks for help. "You can teach them how to read, Rosie," he says. "You read very well."

Rosie does not feel confident. She had to practice a lot to learn how to read. The words and letters used to dance in her head.

"But how can I teach them?" she worried.

"Teaching is just as much about love and kindness as it is the lessons. You will find a way, Rosie," Farmer Jack assures her.

Farmer Jack helps the reindeer out of the trucks and settles them in the warm barn for the night.

"You and Rosie have been very kind to us," says Trey. "Thank you."

Farmer Jack returns to Rosie, leans down, and smiles. "Stay calm. You can do this. Be patient with yourself and with them. I have faith in you. Start with the big letters first. Add pictures too."

Rosie relaxes a little. She trusts Farmer Jack.

The next morning, Rosie gathers the farm animals.

"I need your help," she tells Nancy, the prize-winning goat.

"I have to teach our reindeer friends how to read, but I need you to tell them your story. Will you do that?"

"Of course," says Nancy.

"George, your help is needed too," says Rosie to the draft horse.

"Anything you need," he tells her.

"Please gather all the animals and help me get any fruit that is stored in the cellar. Vegetables too."

George smiles. "You want to feed them?"

"No, I want to show them what they are reading and spelling."

"That is genius!"

The animals return soon with more fruits and vegetables than Rosie had expected. They meet Nancy in the barn where she set up a small classroom to include an old chalkboard Farmer Jack found in the basement.

The reindeer are waiting with Nancy. They look a little nervous.

"Hi guys," says Rosie. "Let's start by introducing ourselves to each other."

"I'm Trey." "And I'm Dave, his brother."

"I'm Derek,' offers the shy one.

"And my name is Katie. I'm Derek's sister.

Rosie nudges Nancy forward to tell her story. She suspects the reindeer might be nervous about getting help from strangers.

"When Farmer Jack found me, I had a broken ankle that wouldn't heal. I was afraid I wouldn't be able to help here on the farm. I didn't want to disappoint Farmer Jack," explains Nancy. "Rosie was my first friend. She and the other animals helped me to get strong again. Now, I win prizes in the county fair every year." The reindeer start to relax. "You are in good hands here on Callahan Farm, I promise!"

Rosie starts with the basics – the alphabet and simple words. The reindeer feel more and more confident each day.

Rosie teaches them how to write. Nancy and the other animals cheer them on as they copy a new sentence that contains all the letters in the alphabet. "Santa will be so proud of us!" chimes Katie.

the quick brown fox jumped over the lazy

The reindeer continue working hard, practicing every chance they can. Derek practices copying addresses to read aloud, while Dave practices putting names in alphabetical order. Even though Santa uses GPS now, they don't want to take any chances that anyone will be missed.

Finally it is time for the reindeer to return to the North Pole. Rosie, Farmer Jack, and all the animals gather to say good-bye. Trey steps forward with a note. "We'd like to read something aloud to you all," explains Trey.

Trey, Dave, Katie, and Derek take turns reading the letter with confidence. They share funny stories from the week as well as a list of reasons they are grateful. They are so excited to return home to tell Santa all about their experience on Callahan Farm!

Rosie's heart is full as she says good-bye to her new friends.
With a nod toward Farmer Jack, she realizes that, in helping
others, she also learned a lot about herself.

"Maybe that's the true magic," thinks Rosie.

And she smiles.

About the Author

I didn't plan on becoming a book author for young children. Honestly.

I retired from the Air Force, spent 15 years as a classroom teacher, and now run my own company that has nothing to do with either, but I do love to write! Always have.

Rosie was the one who found me. While doing some research for my business, I realized that I couldn't find any farm trucks for girls. Sure, we all know that boys and girls have so many creative options in their toy arsenals today – more so than any other time in history – but I wanted something just classically pink and girly … and I couldn't find it. So .. I created her!

I hope you have fun reading about Rosie's adventures as much as I've had fun creating her and her friends.

For study guides and additional resources, as well as my other publications and special bonuses, visit www.facebook.com/scoutandcompanypublishing/.

Contact me at scoutandcompanyflorida@gmail.com. I'd love to hear from you!!

Made in the USA
Columbia, SC
22 February 2022

56380102R00020